ENCHAN

& THE MAGIC
OF SHADOWS,
BOOKS AND POWER

Written By

Saif Rafique

"Enchantments & The Magic of Shadows, Books and Power," published through Young Author Academy.

Young Author Academy LLC

Dubai, United Arab Emirates

www. youngauthoracademy. com

ISBN: 9798728319689

Printed by Amazon Direct Publishing.

Dedicated to Amina,

the most kind-hearted,

caring mother ever.

Contents

PROLOGUE

Greetings. I am the Story Keeper.

When I welcome visitors inside my "ETERNAL GRAVEYARD" house, they will usually tell me the most demonic and scary tales. Tales of adventure and bravery.

Our first guest is a short middle-aged knight who was known for his risky actions, all to save his kingdom.

I remember the moment when this peculiar man sat on my couch, awaiting to hear his horrible story to begin.

Keep reading…   IF YOU DARE!!

Chapter One

The Beginning of a New Adventure

A Story by Calci.

It all began at home.

It was 4am in the morning and I couldn't sleep. I could not even close my eyes, yet I was so tired that I felt paralyzed.

Oh! I forgot to introduce myself...

... My name is Calci. I have emerald green eyes, a pointy nose and a brown, but slightly grey moustache.

I have an oval boney face with wrinkles. My nails are encrusted with dirt and I have a long scar on my left cheek.

I usually wear layers of glimmering gold armour to protect myself from vile threats. Vile threats, you ask? Well, they would typically come in the form of this type of adventure.

My father, Sulvai, died in war two years ago...

I don't want to brag too much, but I am known for my bravery and determination to save my Kingdom. I'm kind-hearted and courageous and I'm what you call, a brave hero.

BACK TO MY STORY...

I stumbled out of bed silently whining to myself until breakfast.

DING-DONG!
The doorbell rang. I splashed my face with some freezing cold water to refresh myself.

Next I walked, but not stumbled, to the door. Upon opening the door, there stood one of King Albera's servant.

"King Albera needs you immediately! Go to his Palace!" he demanded.

I was quite confused, but nevertheless, I knew that I had to follow the King's orders. I ran to the King's Palace and I noticed, standing there outside the palace was the King, himself. He was waiting for me.

"Some explorers were lost, looking for a thousand year-old creature in 'The Forest of Eternal Darkness' and I need you to find them!" he said with a worried tone.

The King gave me a map from the Kingdom. It showed the way to 'The Forest of Eternal Darkness.'

"While there is blood in my veins, I will find them, I promise," I vowed whilst bowing to the King, upon hearing his orders.

"Good-bye!"

I ran to the forest as fast as lightning, following the map very carefully to ensure that I was following the correct way. I ran for half an hour, but it felt like I had been running for a thousand hours.

Chapter Two

The Forest of Eternal Darkness

Finally, upon finally reaching the forest, I knew why it was called, 'The Forest of Eternal Darkness.' It was quite dark inside, and amongst the trees, there were frightening kinds of things, like plants that had mouths and razor sharp teeth! But that's for another adventure.

I hastily ran further into the forest and saw that the trees were all lined up in a row, but they were also far apart.

They appeared like a crowd of jet-black coats. It was at this point, I thought I might never find them!

I had no idea where they were and I was so hungry that I could faint. Maybe I really will faint! I remembered how King Albera had trusted me to go on this mission, and how he expected me to succeed, so satisfying my hunger would just have to wait.

The grass was getting taller and taller, and I realized that soon I wouldn't be able to see. I kept running until the grass was taller than me. I couldn't see my own hand! I had to keep running, and so that's what I did.

Luckily, for some strange reason, the grass started to become shorter again! Even luckier, I stumbled across some footprints! I followed their trail. I believed that they could definitely belong to the missing explorers. The footsteps led to a cave that looked like it was about to collapse! I watched my step and carefully walked into the cave.

There in front of me, I noticed that there were boulders lying on the bumpy ground. I then came across three tunnels and I thought, 'Which one should I choose? Choosing the wrong tunnel may be disastrous.'

I ended up walking into the second tunnel. Surprisingly, the ground wasn't bumpy anymore. All the other walls including the ceiling were bumpy though! I started running as fast as I could.

My eyes widened, I was so shocked!! I had achieved my goal and there inside the cave stood the missing explorers! I approached the missing men.

I told the explorers, whose names were AJ, Joe and Dan, "You are going to be safe now."

Chapter Three

Wakey, Wakey, Big Mistakey

The explorers were very happy and they told me that they had discovered and investigated the tunnel and they revealed that under the rock on my left foot, there was an ancient artefact.

I, along with the help of all the explorers' help, lifted the huge rock and there indeed, underneath was an ancient book. Pretty weird, huh?

I looked closer at the book, and on the front cover it read…

'MAGIC SPELLS! ONLY WITCHES,
WIZARDS AND HEROES CAN USE AND
TOUCH, OR YOU WILL RECEIVE AN
ELECTRIC SHOCK.'

This was too big to believe. Could I really use magic and spells? There was only one way to find out. I flipped through the book and found a spell.

It read **'TELO HOME SPELL'**

I read further and the magic spell book uncovered its power...

… "Teleport you to your home!"

I tried it, "Bring me home with a big flash, but never a big, huge bash."

It worked! There we were; The explorers and I. Right back in the middle of the kingdom. It didn't take long for us to realize that a man with shadow powers was taking over the kingdom. The spell had really worked.

"Calci!" yelled AJ. "You have magic, remember! Use it against Shadow Man!" he exclaimed happily.

"Well... Ok, let's do this!" I replied.

"I will destroy the world! See my true power!" he boomed in a dark, vile and demonic voice.

"Be quiet!!!" I screamed back. WOW! He actually obeyed and went quiet!

"I will beat you! I am a wizard!" I told him.

"Very well, I challenge you to a "Booto-Kai'!" he said.

"What's a Booto-Kai?" I asked him.

Well.... I knew that asking a villain was kind of weird, awkward and embarrassing, but I did not know what it was.

"Booto-Kai is the legendary battle between good and evil," he answered.

"Fine! Let's do this!" I shouted.

Chapter Four

The Legendary Battle

Part 1

I quickly flipped through the book of spells and there on page 1,152, I found a spell called SHAD-20.

I read on and found out that it had the power to destroy all shadows for a period of twenty minutes.

THIS WAS IT! He will be powerless for twenty minutes, which will give us enough time to beat him.

I then *read* the spell out loud. "Shadows, shadows disappear, in twenty minutes you will reappear."

It worked! Except that it also worked on us. Let me get this straight... I read the spell and all shadows suddenly disappeared...

Including ours. So basically, every-one was frozen in place for the next twenty minutes.

I thought of asking a villain, 'What was the most embarrassing thing that can happen to you?' ...but this was way worse.

Twenty minutes past and the battle continued. I found a spell that was pretty strange *if you ask me*.

RE-SPELL-START.. *What it does*: DESTROY ALL EVIL AND MAKE YOUR DAY GO BACK TO NORMAL, IN ORDER TO DO THIS, SAY THE SPELL BUT YOU MUST MAKE A SACRIFICE."

"Shadow Man, can you start attacking again tomorrow?"

"Fine!" The Shadow Man boomed. It was, after all, a Thursday in January of 2023. It was the day, the year and the month where Shadow Man possessed his strongest powers.

I used my last free day to look at and memorize every spell in the book by using a spell of *super speed.*

Chapter Five

The Legendary Battle

Part 2

Because I read the entire spell book and memorized the spells and power moves, I now knew all of the spells in the universe and I was convinced that I could now beat Shadow Man.

That was when Shadow Man arrived. It was 4 pm in the afternoon.

"Let's do a Booto-Kai!" He roared furiously like a raging lion.

"I accept!!!" I replied.

I was ready! I was about to enter the legendary battle of good and evil!

"The Booto-Kai will start in 5, 4, 3, 2, 1... GO!!!" Shadow Man yelled.

The Shadow Man formed a shadow hologram of himself that appeared like you could feel with your bare hands. It made a floating ball of a shadow and threw it at me. I dodged it, but like a boomerang it came back, not to him, but rushing towards *me*.

I quickly remembered the reverse-spell that I had memorized, so I recited it,

"Bring it back to you, and not to me,
also bring him a honey bee."

"What's that supposed to mean?" Shadow Man asked, in curiosity.

Suddenly, the shadow ball came rushing towards him with amazing speed and hit him. Next, a honey bee came out of nowhere, stung him and WOOSH! He vanished!

I used the poison spell on him, but before I had the chance, he made more than 999,999,999 shadow holograms of himself.

How was I going to beat that!

I then quickly remembered the spell of self-duplication and then read it out loud,

> "Duplicate myself more than
> 100 billion times and poke him
> with some dimes!"

Diamonds and dimes hit Shadow Man, but he dodged them all. All of a sudden, I felt a little tingle and then I started to feel weird. Ok, now the tingle started to become very, very strong. I then began to duplicate. 952,849...   952,850... There are so many of me! Suddenly, I had an army of myself!

The self-duplication spell worked!

"Destroy him!!!" I ordered the army.

Each of them were taking on one Shadow Man as I took the real one. I used a SPELL OF PROTECTION as a shield. It would last for three minutes.

I thought about the RE-SPELL-START spell and how you had to make a sacrifice. I figured out that it was the only way to stop him. I had to do it! Not the sacrifice, the spell. *But who would want to make a sacrifice?*

I ran to the explorers and asked them, "Someone here has to make a sacrifice, who will it be???"

Joe accepted the mission and said that he would do it.

CHAPTER SIX

DID IT WORK??

One problem though, how would we make the sacrifice?

"I think I should set him on fire with my magic," I requested.

Well I know that sounds straight-up weird, but it was the only way I could think of.

"Ok!" Joe replied.

"I'm so sorry I have to do this," I told him.

"It's ok, and it's meant to be like this," he understood and said sadly.

I read the spell,

"Fire, Fire go on him and burn him,

also smash him with a rim."

And with that, his hands, his face, his body, and his everything else began to set on fire.

Just like the honey bee, a basketball rim appeared out of thin air, smashed him and then vanished. I know your big question right now, it's, '*Did it work*???'

Well, you're about to find out! I looked directly at Shadow Man and slowly, very slowly, his shadow holograms were disappearing. Except one thing was wrong, Shadow Man was still there.

Ok! Now I know you're thinking '*how*?'

Shadow Man used his powers but nothing happened.

"What, there's something wrong with my powers! Come on powers, why aren't you working!!??" Shadow Man hollered.

That's when I realized the sacrifice, it destroyed Shadow Man's powers!

"Shadow Man! You're powerless, now get out of this kingdom!" I demanded.

Shadow Man ran out of the kingdom with tremendous speed.

The next day I gathered almost ten thousand people to listen to my announcement.

"Ladies and gentlemen, can I please have your attention? Yesterday, you might have thought I had saved the kingdom from a dangerous threat, but that's only half true. Without the help of three explorers named AJ, Joe and Dan, the kingdom would have been destroyed. They helped me save the kingdom. Fortunately, Joe needed to make a sacrifice for all of us. He was a worthy friend to us.

He was brave and courageous to take huge risks. We will always remember him!"

"Whoo, great speech!" the crowd shouted.

"Don't give cheers just to me. AJ and Dan, come onto the stage."

AJ and Dan marched to the stage happily, ready to receive applause from the crowd.

"Now give a big cheer to AJ and Dan!!!"

"WOOHOO, YOU'RE AWESOME!" the crowd roared.

All of us bowed and then got off the stage. All of a sudden, The ground began to tremble, a colossal spider with large rhino horns and a huge pointy tail burst out of the ground!

"This is the creature we were looking for. The BLINDING WIDOW!" he told me, sounding surprised.

"I have to fight this thing?! This is a crazy adventure for me…"

UNTIL MY NEXT TAIL-TWITCHING

STORY!

GOODBYE FOR NOW…

CALCI.

Chapter Seven

The BW's Recap and Return

If you don't remember what happened last time, here's a recap…

I found some missing explorers trapped in a cave where they had stumbled across an enchanted spell book.

I became a wizard to protect my kingdom from Shadow Man…

…and a huge spider with a tail, claws and rhino horns burst out of the ground, conquering our kingdom.

So here I am now, fighting this colossal beast!

The BLINDING WIDOW (BW) had its claws ready with a speedy slash. First, it slashed me, lucky for me, I dodged it. Next, it charged straight towards AJ. When he reached AJ, he stopped. Suddenly, he used his pointy claws and clenched AJ. AJ was still alive though at this stage, but then there was a strange voice, more like a dark whisper…

…the dark whisper was coming from the spider, and …. only AJ could hear it.

"I used the poison clench claw on you, in twenty-four minutes, you will be my servant..." the dark voice whispered to AJ.

"Set a timer for twenty four minutes... NOW!" AJ told me, sounding frightened. So I did. I set a timer for 24-minutes on my smart watch.

"Why? What will happen in 24 minutes?" I asked AJ.

"I will become a servant for the spider. Poison is spreading through my veins and I only have 24 minutes until the poison clench claw affects me fully!"

"What!? The BW has some kind of power move called the poison clench claw?"

All of this was true. BW scuttled up to the first person it saw and looked him right in the eyes... The person, whose name was TJ suddenly stopped getting scared, stopped moving and entered a trance: seeing a possible glimpse of the future. In the trance, TJ saw that the spider had an army of servants ready to attack. Then as fast as he was put there, TJ was not in the trance any more.

But guess what?! The spider still wasn't done yet! The spider's tail then began to glow, turning it into a glimmering silver kind of colour. I hit its tail with my sharp sword.

What?! I didn't even make a scratch! That glow must have turned his tail into some sort of impenetrable metal.

But even now, the spider still wasn't finished with it's unpredictable mischief yet!

BOOM! Finally the BW raised its frightful legs and stomped so powerfully that somehow it created a small mountain in front of it bouncing me, along with TJ away.

Chapter Eight

Six Minutes Left!

"Only... six... minutes... leeef... t," AJ moaned, sounding extremely weak.

"Come on AJ, stay with me, stay with me. Try to hold it for a tiny bit longer," I told him sounding worried. The BW ran to TJ once again and this time, it wasn't to give him the trance.

It was worse! BW gave TJ the poison clench claw! Again the spider's voice came to its victim. All of a sudden, The BW began running around giving people the poison clench claw!!!

"There are only six minutes left for everyone who got the poison clench claw spell, including the people who just got it!"! AJ told me.

"OH-NO!!!" I replied.

The spider had one last trick up its sleeve. It duplicated himself, but the other versions of him were different colours. I thought about freezing them all to ice, so I used the SPELL OF FREEZE-POWER.

"Some creatures are green, some creatures are blue,

I'm cool and now, so are you!"

I now had ice power and all the spiders were frozen in impenetrable ice. Except...

...the real blinding widow made a stone mountain again, to protect itself from the freeze-spell. I couldn't beat it. "I can't... do... this..." I whispered to myself. I know it's strange but AJ heard my whisper somehow and said, "You can do this... I know you can... it's about to happen..."

"NO, NOT. NOW....Goodbye Calci..."

"Goodbye AJ," I replied, with a tear running down my cheek.

You won't believe it! But the spider then covered every single victim it had PCC'ed (Poison Clench Claw) with its legs! I know it's a weird thing to do, but just in case, I was just going to wait a bit to see if they come out.

I was waiting... waiting... waiting. Finally they emerged, but their eyes were dark black just like the blinding widows'. Strangely, they all shape-shifted into a...

Wait! What? They are all rhinos...

...now all elephants...

...now all lions...

...now all tigers...

... and now they are back in their normal forms!

Chapter Nine

I Can't Fight My Friends

I can't fight my friends. I give up. I can't do this...

"Yes you can," a voice said.

I looked around, but there was not a human in sight, unless you counted the servants. I wondered if I could speak to this strange voice, so I said, "Who are you?"

I then saw a blur... the blur was a human shape, taller than me. It was getting clearer and clearer. When my eyes adjusted to the blur, I could see it, I could see what was in the blur.

He, a human. It was a real human, not a servant. I immediately recognized him, it was. It was…

…My father. I was speechless.

"Father, is it truly you?!" I asked in curiosity.

"Yes, it's me," he replied.

I tried to hug him as hard as I could! But somehow, my hands went straight through him." I am a ghost, but I came here to give you the power to defeat this huge beast!" he announced.

"OK give me that power then, father!" I asked him.

"There are steps. First, you must find a weak-spot on him. Next, hit it with your sword. Finally, it will know who is boss and he will return to his home, and never come back," Sulvai said.

'Ok! First, find it's weak spot,' I thought.

I ran around the beast about five times and found its weak spot. It was under his eighth eye. It looked like a small green glowing drop of blood sticking to the BW' s skin. It has to be his weak spot, it just has to. I jumped up and hit this beast in its weak spot.

Somehow, nothing happened.

"Dad, how come nothing is happening???" I asked Sulvai.

"You must go to 'The Forest of Eternal Darkness', find the infinity sword, and use its power to destroy this monster!"

Crazy huh?!?!

"OK father, I will complete this task," I replied.

I again ran to the forest even faster than before, probably 50,000 times faster. Already halfway there, I was drenched with sweat. I was a swamp. I still hadn't eaten since my last adventure!

I couldn't stop thinking about my friends. I have to reach the forest and find the infinity sword, then everything will go back to normal.

I ran and ran and ran to the forest. Finally, I reached the Forest of ED (Eternal Darkness). I was absolutely clueless as to where the sword was. I then ran further into the forest and... oh no!

Do you remember those plants with mouths and razor sharp teeth, and how I said that that's another adventure.?.?.?

Ya.. that was this adventure.

They grew probably a billion meters taller then before; a billion times stronger, and a billion times more of them. I have to fight these?!?

I got my sword ready to slash all objects that got in the way. I slashed one vine, but guess what? Two more vines grew out of that spot in no time flat.

CHAPTER TEN

THE GUARDIANS

… If I sliced a vine, they just duplicate!

I couldn't fight this thing. I had to get that sword to save the world. If you're thinking, 'It's only the kingdom,' it isn't! That's because BW might give everyone the poison clench claw and probably have nine hundred and ninety nine trillion people in it's army.

I have to stop that from happening. Anyway, I couldn't figure out how to beat these monstrosities. Suddenly, I had a brilliant idea!

I know this sounds weird, but I think slicing their teeth is their weakness.

Ya, I know that sounds weird and sudden, but it was the only idea I could think of. Well it was worth a try.

'SLICE!, SLICE!, SLICE!'

Finally, I sliced every single tooth on that plant-beast.

Wow! It looked absolutely disgusting!!!

"KAP!" A plant bit me, but it didn't hurt because they didn't have any teeth anymore.

"SSSD," the plants twisted and turned to make a vine door. I opened it, since I knew they weren't dangerous anymore. My eyes widened. I was speechless... You'll never guess what was behind that door. It was a temple, and the infinity sword was inside.

Do you know how I knew that? It was because on top of the door that led inside the temple, there was a sign that read,

'INFINITY TEMPLE'

Chapter Eleven

The Peculiar Temple Adventure

I opened the door of the temple and found the infinity sword just lying there on the floor. I picked it up, but suddenly, a trap door vigorously opened beneath me!

Phew! at least I still had the sword. And just as I thought I had won, the sword vanished! Not vanished, but more like disappeared.

"AAAAAA OOO!" I fell on some sort of metal floor. As my eyes adjusted, I saw that pointy walls were closing in on me! There was no way of getting out!

Just then, a golden door appeared out of no-where, right in front of me. How strange!

I opened the door, ran in, and then slammed it shut behind me. Then I looked around and saw that I was in a Horrifying Hall of Petrifying Purple Portals! How frightening! Let me tell you, that I was not going in a single one of the portals because I needed to focus on my mission: to find the infinity sword, use it's power to destroy the spider, with no more crazy dangerous adventures for me anymore!

I looked for a door in this huge room, but couldn't find any anywhere. Guess I'll just *have* to go though one of these Petrifying Portals!

Here goes nothing!

Suddenly, I ended up in a room with the infinity sword inside! I couldn't believe my luck! I grabbed the sword, but I fell into a booby trap, and for some strange reason, I still had the sword, held firmly in my hand!

The booby trap led to me getting shot out of the temple! I fell on the ground with a big thump.

'THUMP!'

Even though my head ached, I had to use it to undo the curse of everyone in the world becoming zombie-shapeshifter servants!!! I ran to the kingdom as fast as I could, with all my might and strength for a straight half hour until I finally reached the kingdom.

"Father, I have got the sword!" I announced to him.

"Good! Then strike that beast down!" he replied sounding confident and eager.

"Here goes nothing!"

"ROOOAAARRR!!!!!" the beast screeched as I stabbed its weak spot with the Infinity sword. It hit the ground with a big 'SLAM!' Soon, everyone returned back to normal and were A-OK!

Chapter Twelve

The Recovery

"Do you feel good?" I asked AJ.

"Who's AJ? Who are you? Who am I? Where am I?" AJ questioned in curiosity.

"Don't you remember me? Calci! It's me!" I reminded him.

"Hmm? I don't know where I am, or who you are, or who I am," AJ replied.

Strange! Maybe he lost his memory!

"Your name is AJ, I rescued you from the forest, where in the kingdom, you were a zombie servant and I made you human again. My name is Calci."

"Ooo-Kaaay…" said AJ, sounding hesitant.

All the people who were now servants had their memory erased! Everyone began babbling and asking each other questions. I finally calmed everyone down and stopped asking annoying questions.

Whew! They all returned back to their homes, slightly confused. I didn't really care about it that a lot, I was completely starving! Luckily the King had a, well…..King-sized meal to give to me, and boy was it scrumptious! I ate, and then had to recover! A nice nap and a good night's sleep! I had the rest of a lifetime vacation!

Strangely, the sky turned black within two seconds. Even more strange were the huge multi-colored portals. They were the size of buildings, opened in the sky! A ninja robot came out of the first portal, then a huge muscular robot appeared running after the ninja, aiming lasers at him.

Next, a walking, talking TV appeared, then a SUPER POWERED ELECTRO-MECHANICAL EEL WITH CRAZY POWERS. A cloud with arms, a black hole that stopped for five minutes and sucked up fifty things.

I was speechless! Nineteen dinosaurs, living flesh! There were also a billion other kinds of things, but telling you about those would take waaaaaaaayyyyyy too long.

I had to defeat all of these... these things, I didn't know what they were! They were destroying houses, buildings and other precious resources! They were smashing, lasering, karatie-ing, stomping, sucking up, and exploding everything!

I got out of my house and have had enough craziness for today!

"WILL ALL OF YOU JUST STOP DESTROYING THE KINGDOM! HASN'T THIS KINGDOM HAD ENOUGH DAMAGE? WILL YOU JUST LEAVE!" I demanded, sounding frustrated and irritated *(which I was)*.

"OK!" All of the unusual creatures replied strangely.

They actually listened! How peculiar!

Chapter Thirteen

A Super Power?

Right then! I stepped onto the road, the only thing not broken, and just as I had taken one step, two trucks came rushing towards me: a truck with toxic waste, and a truck with some sort of nuclear acid.

As I was walking towards them, the two truck's couldn't pull over in time and crashed into me!

'CCCCC-CH-CH-CH- RRRRRRRR- A-PFFFF!' "OUCH!" The muscular robot lifted the trucks and told me I would make it and that now I had super powers.

He also recommended that I should try them out!

Well… here goes nothing!

I tried to lift a building. I could!

I tried to laser a building with my eyes. I could!

I tried to lift my house with my mind. I could!

I could do anything I wanted! I had all the superpowers in the world!!

"I'm unstoppable!!!!" I roared (*But not literally,*) eagerly. I used my powers to re-build all of the city in a flash. I got home, sat on the couch, put my head on the pillow and slept.

I slept for weeks and weeks on my absolutely delightful, comfy couch.

"ZzzzzzzzzzzEEEUUUAAAAHHHHHHH-AAAAAAHHHH," I yawned.

Whew, now I'm active! I ran out my door and greeted my strange part friend, monster buddies.

"Hey guys, whatcha doin'?" I asked.

"NOTHING, JUST SITTING HERE," they all boomed (*in a happy way, that's just the sound of their voices*).

"Oh, hey! I'll build all of you huge monster apartment's, and I'll do it with my super power's so it will be fast……. Done! Go inside and have the time of your life!" I told them.

"WOHOO HOOOOOOOOOOOOOOOO!!!!!!!" They all screamed in a voice so loud, that it broke a few glasses and windows! I was happy that they were happy, after all, they got blasted into this world with no home, and had no idea where they were. But now that has all changed.

I guess even though my life has turned into some sort of video game, I still didn't have any problems.

Ahhhh, I was so relaxed!

But... Without any adventures, I felt a bit bored. No, super bored.

... I was B-B-B-BBOOOOOOOOREDDDDDD..

I know! I'll ask my monster friends!

I ran into their apartment and asked them for an adventure!

"Hey guys! Can you think of a good adventure for me? Not too dangerous, not too easy, and not too medium," I requested.

"Well........ This sounds a bit crazy but...... but..... But.... Can you find out a way to bring us back into our own dimension!?!?!?!?!?"

"Ok, sure!" I replied.

"I'll get right on it!"

"Thank you!!!!!" They boomed hugely.

Well… better get on it! I used my powers to teleport to my house and I'm working on it. To make it take 99 billion times quicker, I used my super speed!

'ZOOOOOOOOOOOOM!!!!!!!!

Whew! This could take hours!

And so it did.

I worked for **hours and hours and hours and hours and hours and hours and hours and hours and hours!**

Chapter Fourteen

The Hard Goodbye

Well, the good news was, that all my adventures were finished!

The bad news is that… that. that that. That. I had to say goodbye to all of my great, kind, caring monster friends…

I walked to my apartment and said, "I'm finished!!! Come down and see my latest greatest invention!!!"

Well, I guess this is goodbye. It's hard to say goodbye sometimes, especially when it's to great friends. I... I ... I. I had to say goodbye...

The monsters scuttled outside and I showed them my creation.

In case you were wondering, the invention was a portal making device a.k.a, the Hyper genetic mutating pulse of Gerodermia = MC square = E and E = MC square, AKA the HGMPP, the hyper-genetic mutating portal pulser.

I flicked the switch and turned it on.

A huuuuuge portal formed by my invention!

It runs out of power quickly so I told them to jump in, 35 monsters a time!

"Goodbye... Goodbye... Goodbye...Goodbye... Goodbye... Good bye...Goodbye... Goodbye... Good bye...Goodbye... Goodbye... Good bye...Goodbye... Goodbye...

..Good bye...Goodbye... Goodbye... Good bye...Goodbye... Goodbye... Good bye...

Goodbye... Goodbye... Good bye...Goodbye... Goodbye... Good bye...Goodbye... Goodbye... Good bye..." I said to all of them as they left.

When they all left, the HGMPP immediately shut down. What power my creation had!

But alas, this was the last of my incredible, unpredictable, crazy, insane adventures of my life!

Goodbye.. Farewell !

BY CALCI

Epilogue

"Ahhh, so this is how your story happened?"

"Yes, indeed! That is what had happened on my three flabbergasting adventures!" said Calci.

Oh, and by the way, Calci just finished telling me his tale, and you probably forgot that he was even telling it! You probably felt like you were *in* his tale! But, what people say is unpredictable and everyone has a wild imagination.

Boy was that tale long! This intriguing tale inspired me to write all about this, and that is the book that you are reading right now.

But like Calci's tale, it's hard to say goodbye sometimes. In the end, you just need to do it.

And just like that, this is the end of the book…

… I have to say goodbye to *you*.

The End.

ABOUT THE AUTHOR
SAIF RAFIQUE

 Saif is an eight year old boy living in Dubai with a passion for reading and a zest for learning.

What started as love for reading has developed into a love for writing and has a myriad of intriguing ideas, mainly in fantasy and adventure stories.

With a fabulously positive attitude for life and learning, Saif called upon his intensely creative imagination and wrote his first book, enabling him to bring many of his original ideas together.

At school, Saif's favorite subject is English and when he is older, he would like to spread the message for all to take better care of the environment and to reduce pollution.

To contact Saif, email,
author.saifrafique@gmail.com

Printed in Great Britain
by Amazon